AF326579

ODETTE

A Fairy Tale for Weary People

AVE MARIA

ODETTE
A Fairy Tale for Weary People

by

RONALD FIRBANK

with four illustrations by

ALBERT BUHRER

ADELAIDE
MICHAEL WALMER
2017

Odette first published as *Odette d'Antrevernes* with another story 1905
This revised version published with these illustrations 1916
This edition published 2017

by

Michael Walmer
49 Second Street
Gawler South
South Australia 5118

ISBN 978-0-6480233-3-3 hardcover

IN ALL THE WORLD
TO
THE DEAREST OF MOTHERS

Odette: A Fairy Tale for Weary People

I

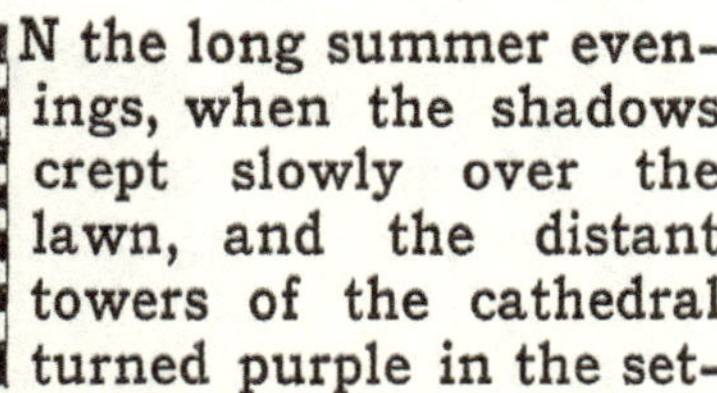I N the long summer evenings, when the shadows crept slowly over the lawn, and the distant towers of the cathedral turned purple in the setting sun, little Odette d'Antrevernes would steal out from the old grey chateau to listen to the birds murmuring "good‑night" to one another amongst the trees.

Far away, at the end of the long avenue of fragrant limes, wound the Loire, all amongst the flowery meadows and emerald vineyards, like a wonderful looking-glass reflecting all the sky;

and across the river, like an ogre's castle in a fairy tale, frowned the chateau of Luynes, with its round grey turrets and its long, thin windows, so narrow, that scarcely could a princess in distress put forth her little white hand to wave to the true knight that should rescue her from her terrible fate.

Just until the sun disappeared behind the trees, veiled in a crimson cloud, little Odette would remain in the shadowy garden, then quickly and mysteriously she would slip back into the old grey chateau ; where, in the long, dim drawing-room, before two wax candles, she would find her Aunt Valerie d'Antrevernes embroidering an altar cloth for the homely lichened village church, that one could see across the rose garden from the castle windows.

" Where have you been, my child ? " her aunt would ask her, glancing up from the lace altar cloth that fell around her in a snowy cloud.

And Odette, in her pretty baby voice, would reply: " I have been listening to the birds saying their evening prayers," and then silently she would sit on a low hassock at her aunt's feet, and tell herself fairy stories until Fortune, her Creole nurse, should come and carry her off to bed.

Sometimes of an evening the old Curé of Bois-Fleuri would come to visit Madame d'Antrevernes, and little Odette would watch them as they talked, wondering all the while if Monsieur le Curé had really seen God. She had never dared ask.

Her aunt always sat in a high arm-chair of faded blue tapestry, embroidered in gold, with the family arms on a background of fleur-de-lys, and her pale, beautiful face, as it bent over the lace altar cloth, made little Odette think of angels and Holy Saints.

Odette had always seen her aunt thus, bending over an altar cloth for

God, so whenever she thought of Madame d'Antrevernes it was with a peculiar reverence that almost approached to awe.

One evening, when little Odette lay awake in her deep four-posted bed, watching the firelight dance upon the strange tapestry figures that covered the walls, she heard Fortune, her old nurse, talking to one of the servants. She caught her aunt's name, then her own, and without realizing that she was doing wrong, she listened to what Fortune said.

She did not really understand what she heard, for she was watching the firelight as it shone upon a tall faded-looking lady in blue, who was regarding with outstretched arms the sky which was full of angels. All about the lady, in a field of red and white flowers, lay sleeping sheep. Her aunt had once told her that the faded-looking blue lady, whom Odette had imagined to be

the Lady Virgin herself, was Joan of
Arc receiving the message from heaven
to deliver France.

So as Odette watched the firelight
dancing upon the faded tapestry, she
listened, without knowing that she was
listening to the voice of Fortune, who,
in the next room, sat gossiping with
another servant.

"She never seems able to forget
him," she heard Fortune say. "Ever
since the day that Monsieur le Marquis
killed Monsieur d'Antrevernes in a
duel, Madame has never recovered."

"She had scarcely been married a
month, sweet soul, when her husband
was brought home to her dead . . .
and so beautiful he looked as he lay in
the great hall, his eyes wide-open and
smiling, just as if he were still alive.
. . . Madame la Comtesse was in the
rose garden at the time with Monsieur
le Curé—no one knew where she was,
and when suddenly she entered the

hall, her hands all full of summer roses, and saw her husband lying dead before her, she gave a terrible cry and fainted straight away. . . . For days after she hung between life and death, and then, when she at last got well again, she always seemed to be thinking of him, always seemed to be living in the past. Sometimes she would sit for hours in the garden staring in front of her, and smiling and talking to herself so that I used to feel afraid. Then, a few years later, when the father and mother of the little Odette were drowned on their way back from India, Madame seemed to wake up from her long dream, as it were, and went to Paris to fetch Mademoiselle Odette from the convent of the Holy Dove.''

Little Odette had fallen asleep berced by the lullaby of the old servant's voice, and when next morning the risen sun shone in a shower of gold through the diamond-paned windows of her room,

THE NURSE'S STORY

and all the birds in the garden below were rejoicing amidst the trees, little Odette had forgotten the conversation she had overheard the previous night as she lay awake watching the firelight dancing upon the faded blue gown of the Maid of France.

OMETIMES of an after-
noon Monsieur le Curé
de Bois-Fleuri would call
at the chateau and ask
Blaise, the long valued
butler, whether Made-
moiselle Odette d'Antrevernes was at
home; and Blaise would smile at
Monsieur le Curé and ask him to be
seated whilst he went to see.

Then slowly, slowly, Blaise would
traverse the great hall, pass under the
torn and faded flags that drooped sadly
like dead things from the massive
rafters and shaking his silver head and
murmuring to himself he would dis-
appear on the great staircase lined with
armour.

And the old Curé would sit musing on the past, his eyes fixed on the torn flags that had once been borne in proud splendour at Pavie and Moncontour.

Then the little Odette in her flowing robe would trip eagerly down the wide oak staircase, and making a low reverence to the Curé, she would take his hand, and together they would walk out into the rose garden that faced the south side of the chateau.

There, by a broken statue on a rustic seat they would sit surrounded by clustering roses, and the Curé, with his soft, low voice, would tell little Odette beautiful stories about the Saints and the Virgin Mary.

But the story that Odette found the most wonderful of all, was the account of the child Bernadette beholding the Holy Virgin in the mountains. This, for her, was the most perfect story in the world, and with her quick, imaginative mind she would picture the little peasant girl Bernadette returning to her parents' distant dwelling, when suddenly in a ray of glorious light, the Holy Mary herself appeared on the lonely mountain path, like a beautiful dream.

Oh! how Odette wished that she could have been little Bernadette! And she would delight to surmise what the little peasant girl looked like; whether her hair was brown, or whether it was gold—and Odette was terribly disappointed when asking the Curé this question, that he only shook his head and said he did not know.

So the days slipped by quietly as on silver wings. Madame d'Antrevernes always in her high blue chair, her altar cloth between her hands, and little Odette on a faded cushion dreaming at her feet.

Then one beautiful evening in August, as little Odette watched the

THE ROSE GARDEN

two twin towers of the distant Cathedral flush purple in the setting sun, and the great round dome of St. Martin's Church loom like a ripe apricot against the sky, a wonderful idea came to her. She, too, would seek the Holy Virgin. She, too, like little Bernadette, would speak with the Holy Mary, the Mother of the Lord Seigneur Christ.

T was the evening of the eventful night. For one whole week Odette had prayed steadfastly, and now this evening she was going to speak to the Holy Mary in the rose garden, when Aunt Valerie and Fortune, Blaise, and Monsieur le Curé were all fast asleep.

She felt terribly excited as she kissed her aunt good-night, and trembling with a beautiful holy fear she allowed Fortune to undress her and put her to bed.

Then for two long hours she watched the moonlight fall upon the dim blue figure of Joan of Arc, for the frail summer fire that Fortune lit of an evening

had long ago burnt itself out, and now
the room was filled with mysterious
shadows and strange creakings of
furniture, so that it was all Odette
could do not to be afraid. At last she
heard the gentle rustle of her aunt's
gown as she passed her door, and
Odette could see the yellow light from
Madame d'Antreverne's candle glint
like a fleeting star through the key-
hole. Soon afterwards she heard the
slow steps of Blaise cross the Picture
Gallery, and then a sudden silence
fell upon the chateau only broken
by faint nocturnal noises from the
garden.

Odette sat up amid her pillows
listening. She felt her heart beating,
beating, as if it were trying to escape.

Then silently she slipped from her
bed, crossed to the window, and looked
out.

Perhaps the Virgin was already
waiting for her in the garden ?

D

But she saw no one.

Far away she could see a few lights shining like fallen stars in the town of Tours, and through the trees upon the lawn she saw the Loire glittering like an angel's robe beneath the moon.

" How wicked to expect the Holy Virgin to wait for me," thought Odette, " It is I that must wait for Her." And fastening a fair silver cross about her neck, she noiselessly opened the bedroom door, and found herself standing alone upon the great dark staircase.

To get to the garden it was necessary to cross the Picture Gallery; for the Picture Gallery was at the top of the great staircase.

Odette trembled as she passed down the long still Gallery where the portraits of her ancestors peered eirily from the panelled walls. But she was comforted by the thought that Gabrielle was at the other end.

It was the picture of Gabrielle

d'Antrevernes, one of the beauties of the court of Louis XIV, that Odette loved most. And she never tired of looking at the long pale face, the sea-blue eyes, and the dull gold hair capped with pearls, of her beautiful ancestress.

Odette adored the tired languid-looking hands, full of deep red roses, that lay like two dead doves upon the silver brocaded gown, and she would weave beautiful tales about Gabrielle, seated on her favourite cushion, peering up at the portrait, her great eyes lost in thought.

But this evening she did not linger as her custom was but with a friendly smile to the beloved Gabrielle she hurried by, her cautious feet all a-pit-a-pat, a-pit-a-pat, on the parquet floor.

Then she went down the broad staircase between the pale armour, beneath the brooding flags, and so to the glass door that led to the garden.

The door was locked, and oh ! the

dreadful creak it gave as Odette turned the key! and a pair of little exploring mice rushed helter-skelter, tumbling about on the slippery floor.

Odette tremulously turned the handle, and suddenly she found herself alone after midnight in the garden.

Her heart beat so that she thought she was going to die. But oh! how beautiful the garden looked beneath the moon! The roses seemed to look more mysterious by moon-shine. Their perfume seemed more pure. Odette bent down and kissed a heavy crimson rose all illumined with silver dew, and then quickly she picked a great bouquet of flowers to offer to the Virgin. Some of the flowers were sleeping as she picked them, and Odette thought, with a little thrill of delight, at their joy on awakening and finding themselves on the Holy Mother's breast.

Then, her arms full of flowers, Odette went and knelt down by the low marble seat, where so often Monsieur le Curé had spoken to her of the Saint Mary and of Jesus, her Son. And there, with her eyes fixed upon the stars, she waited. . . .

In the trees a nightingale sang so beautifully that Odette felt the tears come into her eyes, and then far away another bird sang back . . . and then both together, in an ecstasy, mixed their voices in one, and the garden seemed to Odette as if it were paradise.

Suddenly a low moan, like the sound of a breaking heart, made Odette start to her feet.

Could it be that the Holy Mother was in pain ? She looked about her.

Yes, there it was again . . . a long, low cry . . . it came from the other side of the wall, it came from the road.

Odette hastily collected the flowers in her hands, and ran swiftly down the avenue of lime trees, her untied

hair drifting aerially behind her as she
ran.

Then once upon the white road, she
looked about her expectantly, but there
was no one to be seen. The river ran
the other side of the road like a silver
chain, and far away in the town of
Tours a few lights burnt like candles
in the dark. She stood still, listening
intently ; yes, there again, quite, quite
close, was the long, sad cry.

Odette ran forward to the river bank
from where the sound seemed to come,
and there, her face buried in her hands
—a woman lay.

" Oh! Oh! " cried the little Odette,
the tears rolling down her cheeks, " the
Holy Mother is in pain," and stooping
down, she timidly kissed the sobbing
woman at her feet.

Then as the woman uncovered her
face with her hands, Odette sprang
back with a startled scream. There,
on the grass, amongst the pale-hued

BOIS-FLEURI

daisies, lay a woman with painted cheeks and flaming hair; a terrible expression was in her eyes.

"Who are you? What do you want?" she asked Odette brutally; and Odette, afraid and trembling, began to sob, hiding her face in her hands so as not to see the dreadful eyes of the woman at her feet.

She felt the woman staring at her, though she did not dare look, then suddenly she heard a laugh, a laugh that froze her blood.

"Why, you have no shoes or stockings," said the woman, in a frenzy of mad laughter. "What are you doing here in your nightgown on the high roads? You've begun early, my dear!" And she rocked herself to and fro, laughing, laughing, laughing, and then suddenly her laughter turned to tears. All her poor thin body shook with terrible sobs; it seemed as if her very heart was breaking.

E

Odette uncovered her eyes and looked
at this shattered wreck of a human soul,
and an immense unaccountable pity
seized her, for suddenly she bent down
and kissed the woman on her burning
lips.

The woman's sobs grew quieter, as
she felt Odette's pure cool mouth
upon her fevered face. "Who are
you?" she kept asking her, "Who are
you?"

And Odette in her baby voice whis-
pered back, "The Holy Virgin has sent
me, in order to make you well!"

Presently the woman calmed herself,
and sat staring at the shining river, as
though she had quite forgotten that
Odette was beside her.

"Tell me what is the matter,"
Odette said at length, "and I will try
to help you."

The woman looked at her kindly:
"How should you understand what is
the matter?" she said, "You, who

have lived always with good people, far away from the temptations of the world, what have you to do with the likes of us ? "

" I do not understand," said Odette, looking at the woman with great questioning eyes.

" And may you never understand, little one," said the woman, kissing her. " When I was but a wee mite I heard the preaching folk tell of God and the Angels. You must be one of them, I think ? "

" Oh ! no, Oh ! no," said Odette, " I am not an angel, but I have been sent by the Queen of Heaven to save you here to-night."

The woman looked at her curiously. " You came only just in time," she said, and again her eyes strayed towards the river.

" Let me give you this silver cross," Odette said, changing it from her own neck to the woman's. " Keep it always,

for it is holy, and is a sign that
Jesus came into the world to die
for us.''

The woman took the cross into her
hands, and seemed to weigh it. "Is it
really silver ? " she asked.

Odette smiled at her. " Yes, and is
it not beautiful ? It was given to me
by my mother before she went away to
India; I do not remember her giving
it me, for I was then only a tiny crea-
ture. But Aunt Valerie has often told
me that when mamma hung it around
my neck, she cried, and kissed me, and
told me to love the Holy Vigin, for
that faith, and love, were the only
things that were beautiful in life.''

The woman looked at her sadly. " I
will keep it in memory of you, little
one," she said, "It may bring me
luck," and she got up as if to go.

" Will you promise never to do
things that the Holy Mary would not
approve of ? " asked Odette, taking the

woman's hand, and gazing earnestly
into her eyes.

"I will try, little one," the woman
said, and she stooped and kissed Odette
passionately; the warm tears falling
from her eyes upon Odette's upturned
face.

Far away in the East, the day began
to Dawn. A flush of yellow like ripe
fruit spread slowly across the sky.
The birds in the trees piped drowsily
to one another, and the bent cyclamens
by the river-side lifted their fragrant
hearts in rapture to the rising sun.

The woman and Odette stood side by
side watching the breaking day, then,
as a clock struck away across the
meadows from some church tower, the
woman shivered, and looked down the
long white road that followed the river
bank.

"I must go," she said.

Odette looked at her. "Where to?"
she asked.

"I don't know," answered the woman. "I am going to try to find work—honest work," and taking Odette in her arms she kissed her again and again. "Good-bye, little one," she said, "And since you pray to the Holy Mother, perhaps sometimes you will pray for me."

And then, with a tired, sad step, the woman walked slowly away down the long white road, her shadow falling beside her as though it were her soul.

"Oh, Holy Virgin, Mother of Our Lord Seigneur Christ, I thank Thee for having brought me here this night," prayed the little Odette. "Take into Thy protection, dear Mother, this poor woman who has need of Thee, and bring her safely to Thy beautiful Kingdom in Heaven, for the sake of our Lord Jesus. Amen."

Then little Odette returned thoughtfully to the great grey chateau. And as she passed down the avenue of overarching limes a thousand thrushes sang deliriously amidst the branches.

But Odette felt somehow changed since last she passed the castle gates. She felt older. For suddenly she realized that Life was not a dream; she realized for the first time that Life was cruel, that Life was sad, that beyond the beautiful garden in which she dwelt, many millions of people were struggling to live, and sometimes in the struggle for life one failed—like the poor woman by the river bank.

And Odette turned as she walked, and looked behind her, to where, by the roadside, and dying beneath the golden sun, the red roses that she had gathered for the Holy Mother, shone in the morning light like drops of crimson blood.